"Pri-son! Pri-son!"
Milly ran along the street,
trying not to hear the children
shouting behind her.

Mum and Nan were sitting in the kitchen
when Milly burst into the room.

"They're saying Dad's in prison," said Milly,
trying not to cry. "I told them he was away working,
but everyone laughed at me!" She stopped as she saw
the scared look on Mum's face.

Nan gave her a hug. "It is true, love. We didn't know
how to tell you."

"What did he do wrong?" asked Milly. "Mum, when's
Dad coming home?"

Mum's voice was very quiet. "He won't be back
for a long time," she said. "He stole something that
didn't belong to him. Nan's going to stay with us to help
look after you and Sam. I'll take you to see Dad as soon as I can."

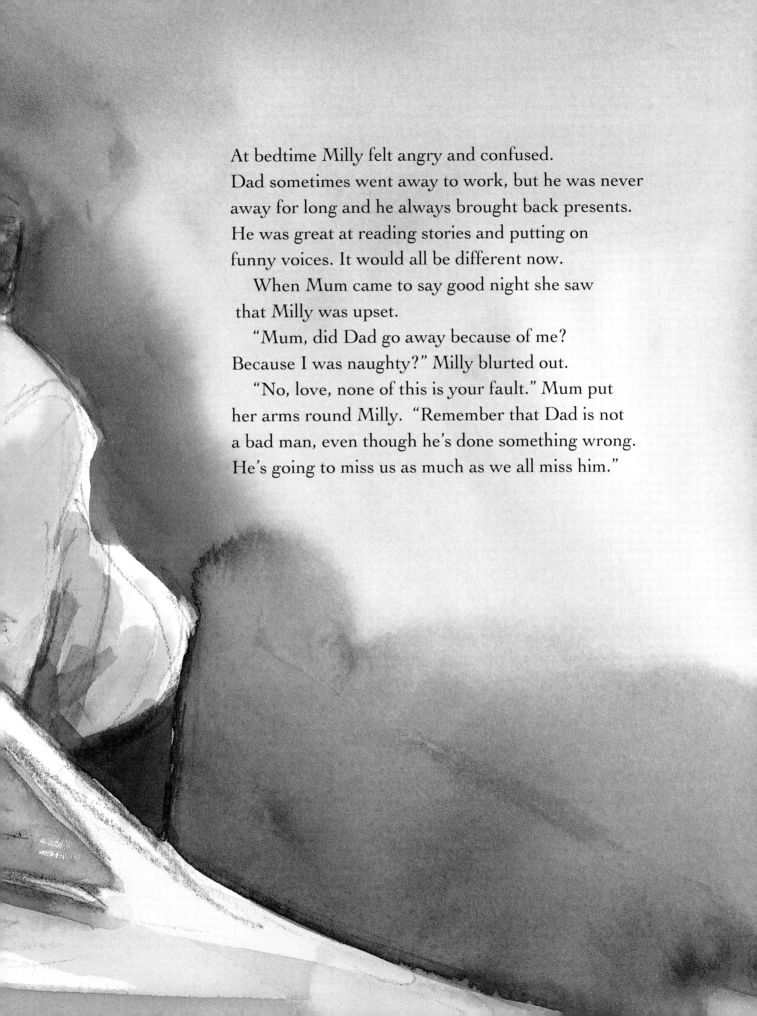

At bedtime Milly felt angry and confused.
Dad sometimes went away to work, but he was never
away for long and he always brought back presents.
He was great at reading stories and putting on
funny voices. It would all be different now.

When Mum came to say good night she saw
that Milly was upset.

"Mum, did Dad go away because of me?
Because I was naughty?" Milly blurted out.

"No, love, none of this is your fault." Mum put
her arms round Milly. "Remember that Dad is not
a bad man, even though he's done something wrong.
He's going to miss us as much as we all miss him."

Next morning Mum took Milly to school.
Her teacher, Mrs Armstrong, was very kind
and chatted to Mum while Milly hung up her coat.
When the bell rang, Mrs Armstrong spoke
to the whole class.

"Remember at the beginning of term we were talking about looking after each other?" she said. "I don't want anyone in this class to forget that it isn't fair to tease people or call them names. Come and tell me if you hear somebody doing that – and if you are feeling upset you know you can always talk to me."

Milly's face felt hot, as if everyone was looking at her.

That afternoon, Mum went to visit Dad.
It was a long way, and she looked tired
when she got back.

"Dad's really missing you," she told Milly
and Sam. "He wants you to draw him
some pictures. We can send them to him."

So Jenny got to work with her paints
and helped Sam with his crayons.

A few weeks later it was time for Milly and Sam's first visit to the prison. Milly looked up at the huge doors and high walls. It was scary and she held tight to Mum's hand. "Mum, what if Dad's forgotten us?" she asked nervously. "Are you sure he wants to see us?"

"He can't wait, love. He really misses you!"

As they went in, they were searched by a lady, and
they had to leave everything behind –
even Sam's teddy.

Then a friendly dog came
and sniffed them. It tickled!

They waited and waited for Dad to come –
and at last he was brought in.

"Dad!" Milly shouted, jumping up.

It was so good to see Dad, and he gave them all
great big hugs.

Dad told them how much he'd been looking forward
to seeing them. He'd brought in some of Milly's
favourite books. "I chose them specially from the library,"
he said. Then he read some stories to the children
and, just for a little while, it felt like home.

All too soon the visit was over. It was time
for them to go.

Milly tried hard not to cry when Dad said goodbye.
He kissed her and whispered, "Be a good girl. Love you!"

"Love you, Dad," said Milly, hugging him tight.

One week later there was a special surprise.

"Package for you, Milly!" Mum handed her a padded envelope.

Milly tore it open. "What is it, Mum?"

"Dad's made a cd," said Mum, "so you can listen to his voice even though he's away."

Milly played the cd over and over again. There were some great animal stories on it. Sam loved it too because he knew that it was Dad talking.

At Christmas, it was sad putting up the tree
and the decorations without Dad.

Everyone at school was talking about
going to see Santa with their mums and dads.
Milly felt left out.

But Mum had a surprise for her....

It felt strange, going to a Christmas party in the prison.
But it was a real party with juice and sausages and
crisps, and Santa was there too!

When Santa handed out presents, the children
waited for their names to be called out.

"Milly and Sam!"

Shyly, they went up for their gifts.

There was someone taking photos. "Smile!" he said,
and he took a picture of the whole family with Santa.

"I'm going to show it to everyone at school,"
said Milly. "Me with my dad and Santa!"

In the spring, when Mum came home from visiting Dad, she had a big smile on her face.

"Great news! Your dad's coming home next week – on your birthday!"

Milly jumped up and down and hugged Mum. "That's the best present ever!" she said happily.

On the day Dad was coming home, Milly was really excited. She wanted to tell her friends at school, but she was scared about what they might say, so she just whispered to her teacher.

"That's terrific news, Milly. On your birthday, too!" Mrs Armstrong smiled.

After school, Milly couldn't wait to get home.
Very slowly, she opened the front door – and there
was Dad, with Sam on his knee.

"Dad! Dad!" she yelled.

"Happy birthday, Milly!" cried Dad.

Milly hugged and hugged Dad, and he didn't
let go for a long time.

"Milly has been fantastic while you've been away,"
said Mum. "I couldn't have managed without her."

"It's good to be home," said Dad, smiling.

Then Milly gave Dad a big kiss. She knew
this birthday would be her best ever.

For more information and advice about
support for prisoners' families,
the following organisations may be useful:

UK
Action for Prisoners' Families
www.prisonersfamilies.org.uk

Barnardo's
www.barnardos.org.uk

The Ormiston Children and Families Trust
www.ormiston.org

Niacro (Northern Ireland)
www.niacro.co.uk

US
Centerforce
www.centerforce.org

The Offenders' Families Helpline
www.offendersfamilieshelpline.org